AF581086

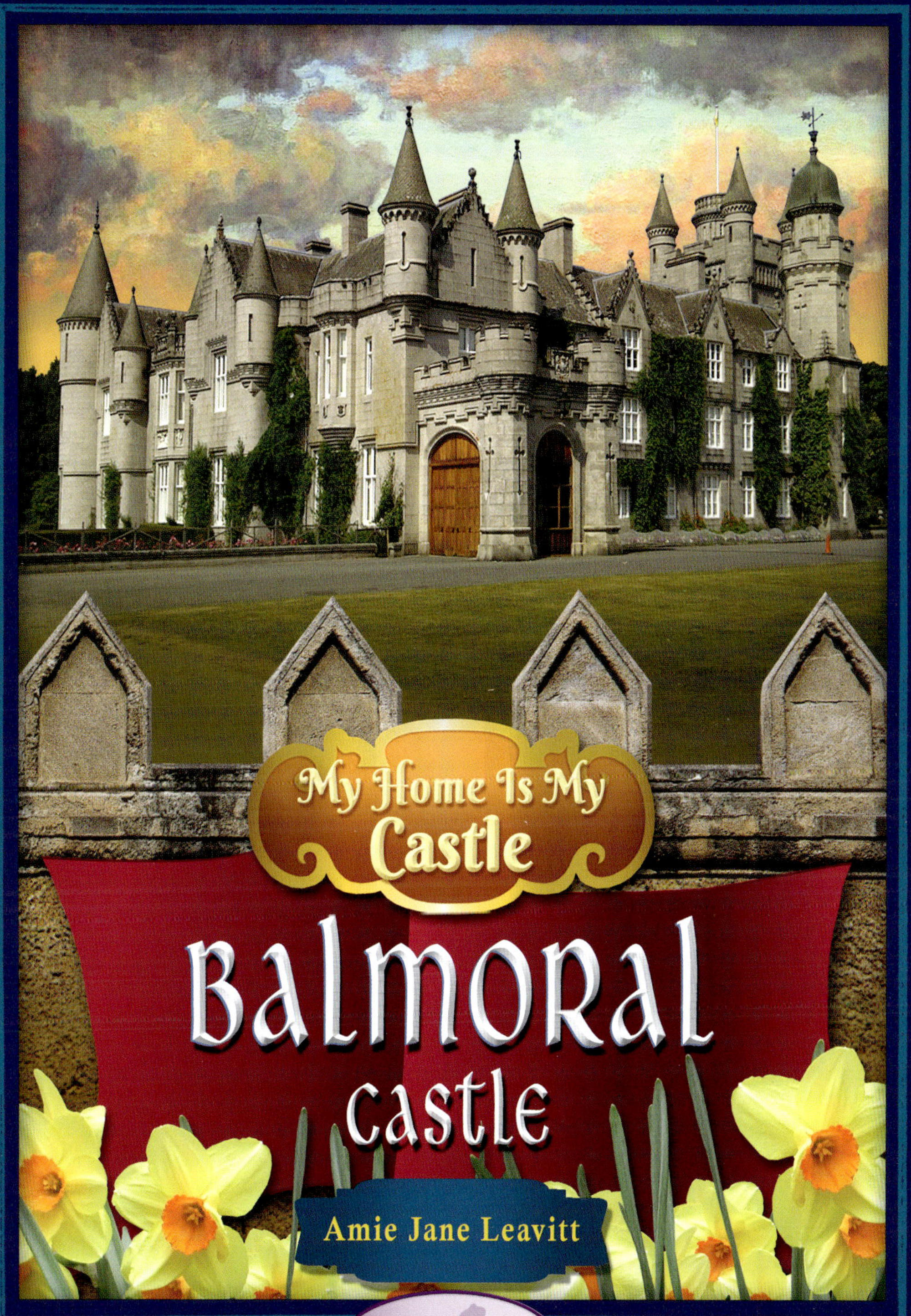

PURPLE TOAD
PUBLISHING

BALMORAL CASTLE by Amie Jane Leavitt
GLAMIS CASTLE by Tammy Gagne
HEARST CASTLE by Ann Tatlock
VERSAILLES by Amie Jane Leavitt
WINDSOR CASTLE by Amie Jane Leavitt

PUBLISHER'S NOTE

The data in this book has been researched in depth, and to the best of our knowledge is factual. Although every measure is taken to give an accurate account, Purple Toad Publishing makes no warranty of the accuracy of the information and is not liable for damages caused by inaccuracies.

ABOUT THE AUTHOR

Amie Jane Leavitt is an accomplished author, researcher, and photographer. She graduated from Brigham Young University as an education major and has since taught all subjects and grade levels in both private and public schools. She is an adventurer who loves to travel the globe in search of interesting story ideas and beautiful places to capture in photos. She has written more than sixty books for kids, has contributed to online and print media, and has worked as a consultant, writer, and editor for numerous educational publishing and assessment companies. Amie particularly enjoyed researching and writing this book on Scotland's Balmoral Castle. She has Scottish ancestry and her family has always been interested in their Scottish roots. Several of her siblings played the bagpipes in their local high school's Scottish bagpipe band and she, herself, played the drums with the band for a short time. Check out her current projects and published works at www.amiejaneleavitt.com.

Printing 1 2 3 4 5 6 7 8 9

Publisher's Cataloging-in-Publication data
Leavitt, Amie Jane.
Balmoral castle / Amie Jane Leavitt.
p. cm.
Includes bibliographic references and index.
ISBN 9781624691362
1. Balmoral Castle (Scotland). 2. Victoria, Queen of Great Britain, 1819–1901—Homes and haunts—Scotland—Highlands. 3. Castles—Great Britain—Juvenile literature. I. Series: My home is my castle.
DA890 2015
914.1
Library of Congress Control Number: 2014946225
eBook ISBN: 9781624691379

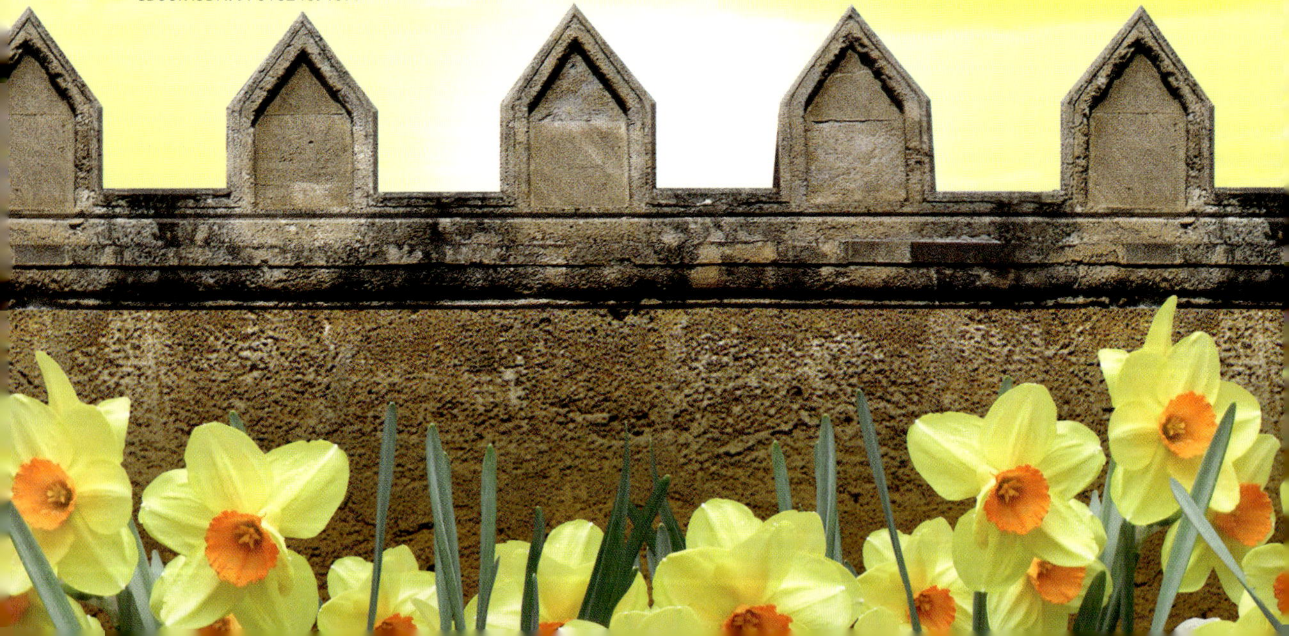

contents

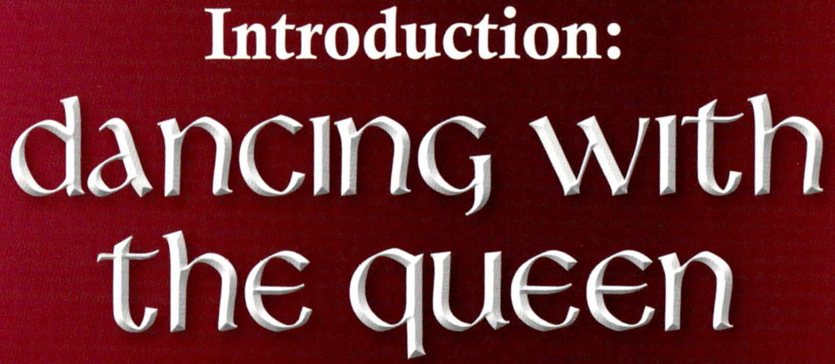

Introduction: Dancing with the Queen

The air is crisp on this fall evening in late September. The leaves have already changed from brilliant green to amber gold and pumpkin orange. Winter in the Scottish Highlands is right around the corner, and soon the trees will be bare and the earth will be covered in a blanket of snow.

Although the weather is getting chilly, the atmosphere in Balmoral Castle is warm and inviting. After all, tonight is the night of the annual Ghillies Ball, a celebratory event that Queen Elizabeth puts on for her family, castle staff, invited guests, and residents of the surrounding villages. This grand affair—which has been a tradition at Balmoral since the days of Queen Victoria—is a way to thank all the people who have helped make the royal family's summer vacation so peaceful and delightful. There are two Ghillies Balls put on every fall—one for each group of staff members who work at the castle during the queen's stay.

Everyone dresses in formal attire for the Ghillies Ball. Ladies dress in long, modest evening gowns with a tartan sash over their dresses. For tonight's ball, the queen wears a floor-length sea-blue ball gown graced with a red tartan sash tied in a rosette at her shoulder. Sparkling gemstones and diamonds on necklaces, bracelets, rings, and tiaras are also the norm for the ladies—especially for the queen. Men dress in suits. Some—including Prince Phillip and Prince Charles—wear formal kilts.[1]

Autumn is a glorious time of year at Balmoral. That's probably why it's the season that the grand Ghillies Ball is held.

Little has changed in the grand ballroom at Balmoral since the 1890s when Queen Victoria resided there.

Tonight's events start with a traditional Scottish dinner prepared by the royal chefs. Many of the vegetables on the menu were grown in the castle gardens, and the royals themselves hunted much of the meat. After the guests have enjoyed the deliciously prepared food, they are invited into the castle's ballroom for the main event. The purpose of the ball is to dance—and dance, they all will. Queen Elizabeth and Prince Phillip, with three other couples, start the dancing with a traditional Highland eightsome reel. The soft glow from the candelabra illuminates the ballroom with a warm golden light. Lively accordion music plays in the background as the dancers twirl, sashay, and move clockwise and counterclockwise around each other in the circle wheel dance.

Following the queen's inaugural number, the rest of the guests are invited to take the floor. As the musicians serenade them with Scottish tunes, the guests dance reels, waltzes, and other traditional numbers well into the evening. It is indeed a time of revelry for everyone and a grand way to end another holiday at Balmoral. When the evening comes to a close, there is a twinge of sadness in the attendees' eyes. Even though the night may be over, they all know that this isn't the end of the happiness at Balmoral. The royal family will be back next year and will bring with them the tradition of the twice-annual Ghillies Ball.

Tradition is of the utmost importance at Balmoral, a favorite retreat of the Windsor family. The Windsors do their best to keep Balmoral just the way it was when it was first built more than 160 years ago by their royal ancestors Queen Victoria and Prince Albert.

The Ghillies' Ball was a favorite of Queen Victoria. She is shown here in 1868 dressed in black in the center of the far right hand side. Once Prince Albert died (in 1861), Queen Victoria always wore black mourning clothing.

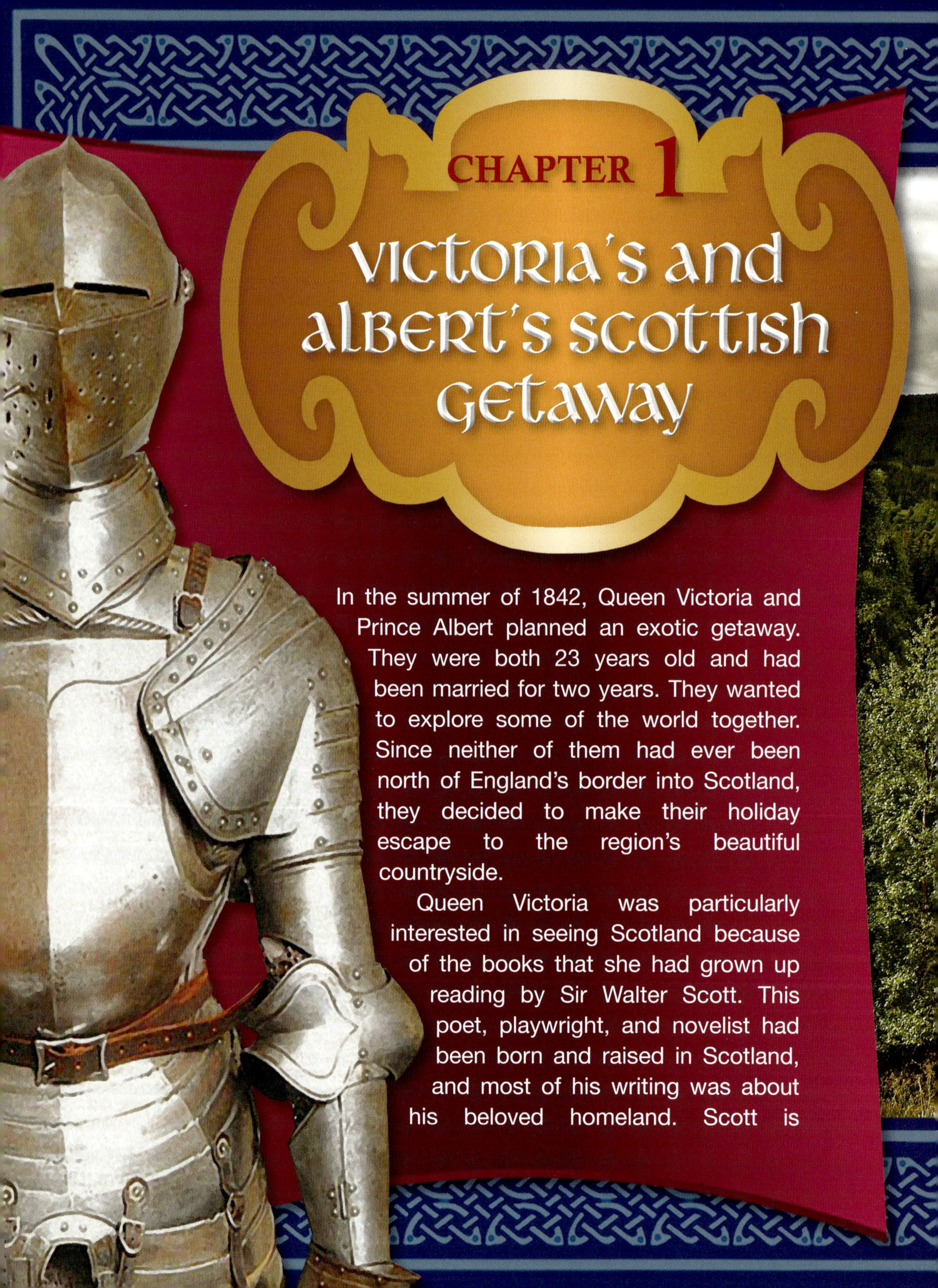

CHAPTER 1

Victoria's and Albert's Scottish Getaway

In the summer of 1842, Queen Victoria and Prince Albert planned an exotic getaway. They were both 23 years old and had been married for two years. They wanted to explore some of the world together. Since neither of them had ever been north of England's border into Scotland, they decided to make their holiday escape to the region's beautiful countryside.

Queen Victoria was particularly interested in seeing Scotland because of the books that she had grown up reading by Sir Walter Scott. This poet, playwright, and novelist had been born and raised in Scotland, and most of his writing was about his beloved homeland. Scott is

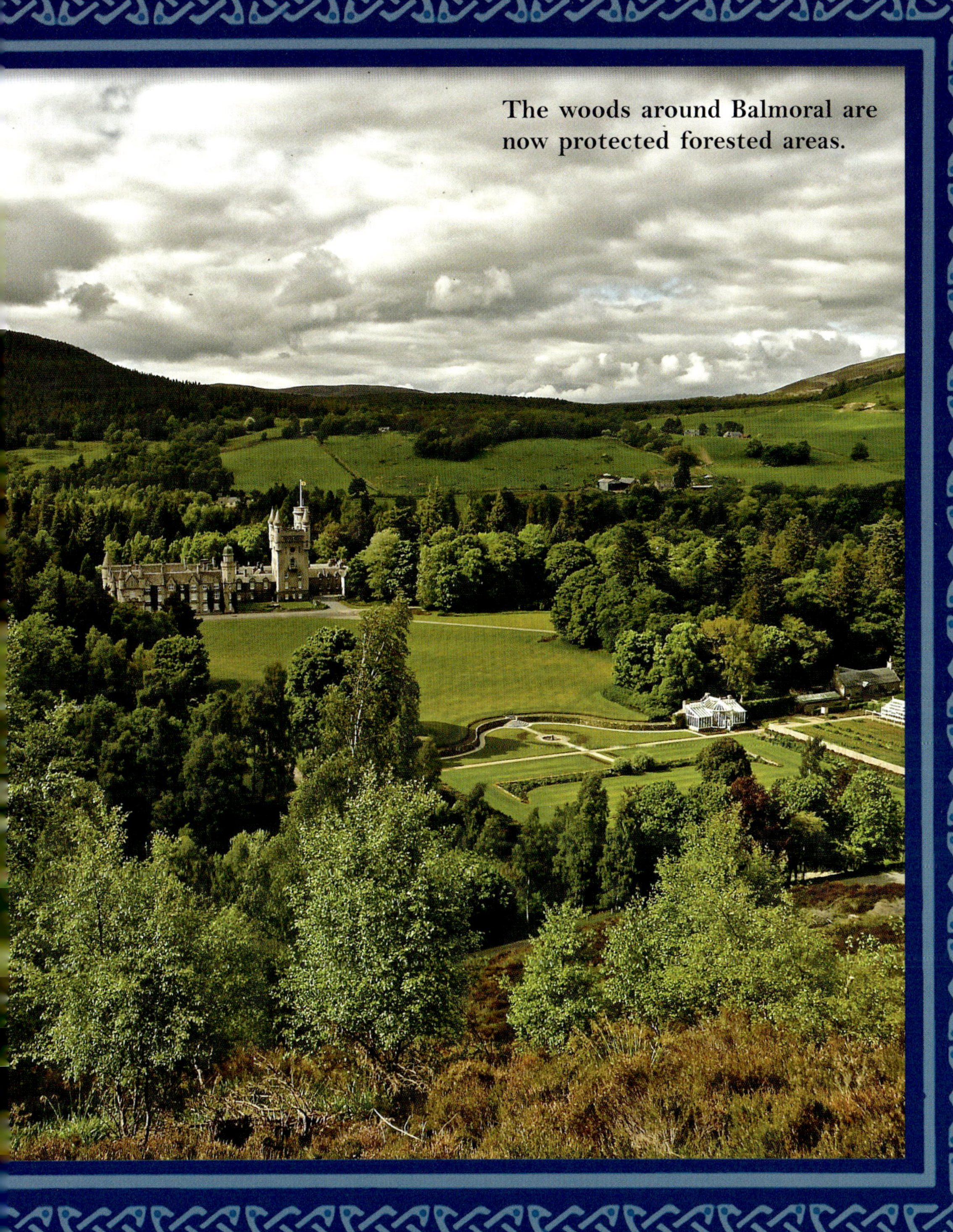

The woods around Balmoral are now protected forested areas.

Sir Walter Scott

famous for such stories as *Waverly, The Lady of the Lake, Rob Roy,* and *Ivanhoe.* In his writings, he described Scotland's beautiful and rugged landscape. He wove into his tales the rich history and unique culture of his people. When Victoria was a young girl, the first novel she read was Scott's *Bride of Lammermoor,* a romantic historical novel set in the Lammermuir Hills in the southeastern region of Scotland. She was enchanted by the stories Scott created and longed to see this charming place for herself.

Prince Albert was also a fan of Scott's works. He had grown up reading them in Germany. He, too, anxiously anticipated seeing these beautiful places with his own eyes.

On August 29, 1842, Victoria and Albert left Windsor Castle for their journey. They traveled by railroad to London and then took a carriage to the Woolwich docks where they boarded a royal ship bound for Scotland. On August 31, they finally neared the Scottish coastline. According to Queen Victoria's journals, the Scottish coast was "very beautiful, so dark, rocky, bold, and wild, totally unlike our [England's] coast."[1] They saw many small fishing boats along the way, and from one of them floated the song of a bagpiper. This was definitely Scotland!

Victoria and Albert finally arrived at their first destination, Edinburgh, Scotland, on September 1. When the pair disembarked at the docks, the Scottish people cheered and applauded. At that time, not a lot of people vacationed in Scotland, so most Scottish people had never even seen anyone from London before. Having the queen and her new husband visit their city was a delight and an honor.

Everywhere Victoria and Albert went on their royal tour, they were greeted with great fanfare. In the Highlands, there were parades, fireworks, dancing, and music. Bagpipe bands in full regalia—kilts, tartan knee socks, sashes, and feather bonnets—marched to the beat of the drums as the pipers droned familiar battle tunes. In the evening by torchlight, Highland dancers high-stepped their routines to perfection. Everywhere, the Scots wore their traditional apparel: the men wore kilts and carried Lochaber axes; the women wore long, flowing dresses with flowers in their hair. Queen Victoria described the scene in her journal:

> The firing of the guns, the cheering of the great crowd, the picturesqueness of the dresses, the beauty of the surrounding country with its rich background of wooded hills, altogether formed one of the finest scenes imaginable. It seemed as if a great chieftain in olden feudal times was receiving his sovereign. It was princely and romantic.[2]

Victoria and Albert were absolutely smitten with Scotland. Albert loved the landscape—the mountains, forests, and open spaces reminded him of places he had known in Germany. He loved to go hunting in the woods and fishing in the clear streams and rivers. Victoria loved everything about the landscape, too—and she was fond of the food, clothing, and culture of the Scottish people. On her first morning in Scotland, she tried the traditional Scottish hot breakfast cereal, porridge, for the very first time and liked it. Scotland was such a contrast from the urban environment of London that Victoria and Albert were able to totally relax and enjoy themselves.

Victoria and Albert at their wedding

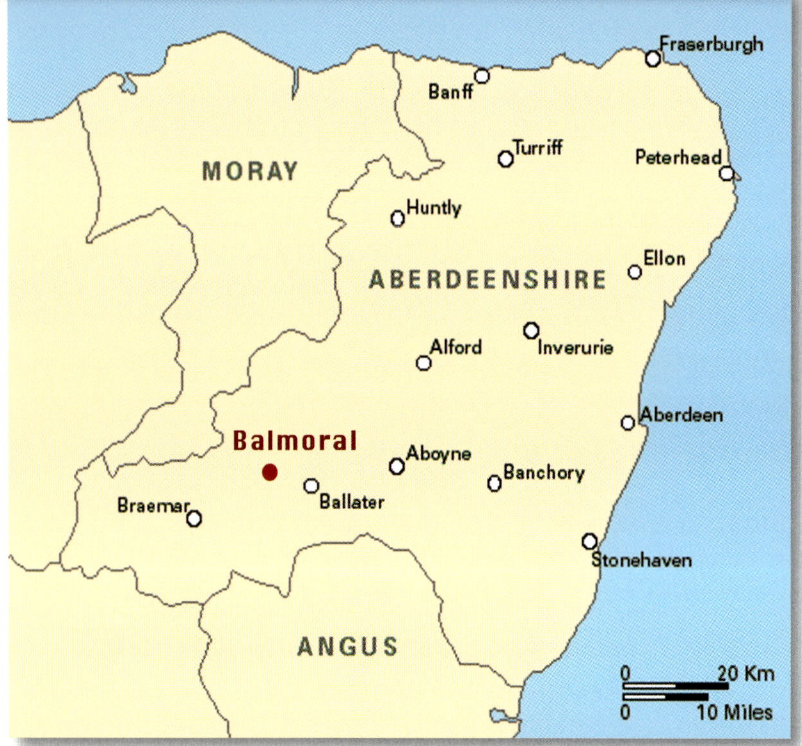

The royal couple returned as visitors to Scotland two more times—once in 1844 and then again in 1847. Finally, they decided they didn't want to just *visit* Scotland; they wanted to live there, for at least part of the year. Prince Albert bought some property in the Highlands as a gift for Victoria. When he did so, Victoria became the first English monarch to have a home in Scotland since Charles I had ruled in the 1600s. Since the royal couple purchased this property with their own funds, it was considered their private property. It remains in this private-land-ownership status even today. If Scotland should vote for independence from the United Kingdom—which it came close to doing in 2014—the royals would still own Balmoral Castle and estate.

The land is in Aberdeenshire along the banks of the River Dee. On the property, there was already a small fifteenth-century castle. It was a delightful place and Albert and Victoria liked it just fine. However, the castle was simply too small. It would never be able to accommodate their family and the entourage that always accompanied them. Victoria and Albert decided to build a new one. It would be named after the castle that was already on the property: Balmoral Castle.

PORRIDGE

Porridge is a traditional breakfast in Scotland, and it is still a popular menu item. Many people in other parts of the world have adopted this dish. It is easy to cook—even a kid can make it with a little adult supervision!

FUN FACT: Traditionalists stir their porridge with a wooden stick called a spurtle. They say it helps the oats cook more evenly. If you don't have a spurtle, try using the handle of a wooden spoon.

Ingredients

3 cups water
¼ teaspoon salt
2 tablespoons brown sugar
1 tablespoon honey
1 cup steel-cut oats
1 cup raisins (optional)
milk, maple syrup, brown sugar, or honey to taste
sliced banana (optional)

Directions

1. Place the water and salt into a pot. **Ask an adult** to help you boil the water on the stove.
2. Once the water is boiling, stir in the oats, brown sugar, and honey. Add the raisins if you want to include them.
3. Turn the heat down to simmer and place a lid on the pot.
4. Let the oatmeal cook for 20–30 minutes. Stir often.
5. Test the oatmeal with a spoon. If it's too chewy, add a little more water and cook a few minutes longer. It should be smooth and creamy. When the porridge is done, take it off the heat and let it sit for two minutes.
6. Scoop some in a bowl. You can eat it plain like this, or you can add a little milk, brown sugar, more honey, or maple syrup to taste. Some people also like it with sliced banana or other fruit on top.

Makes 4 servings

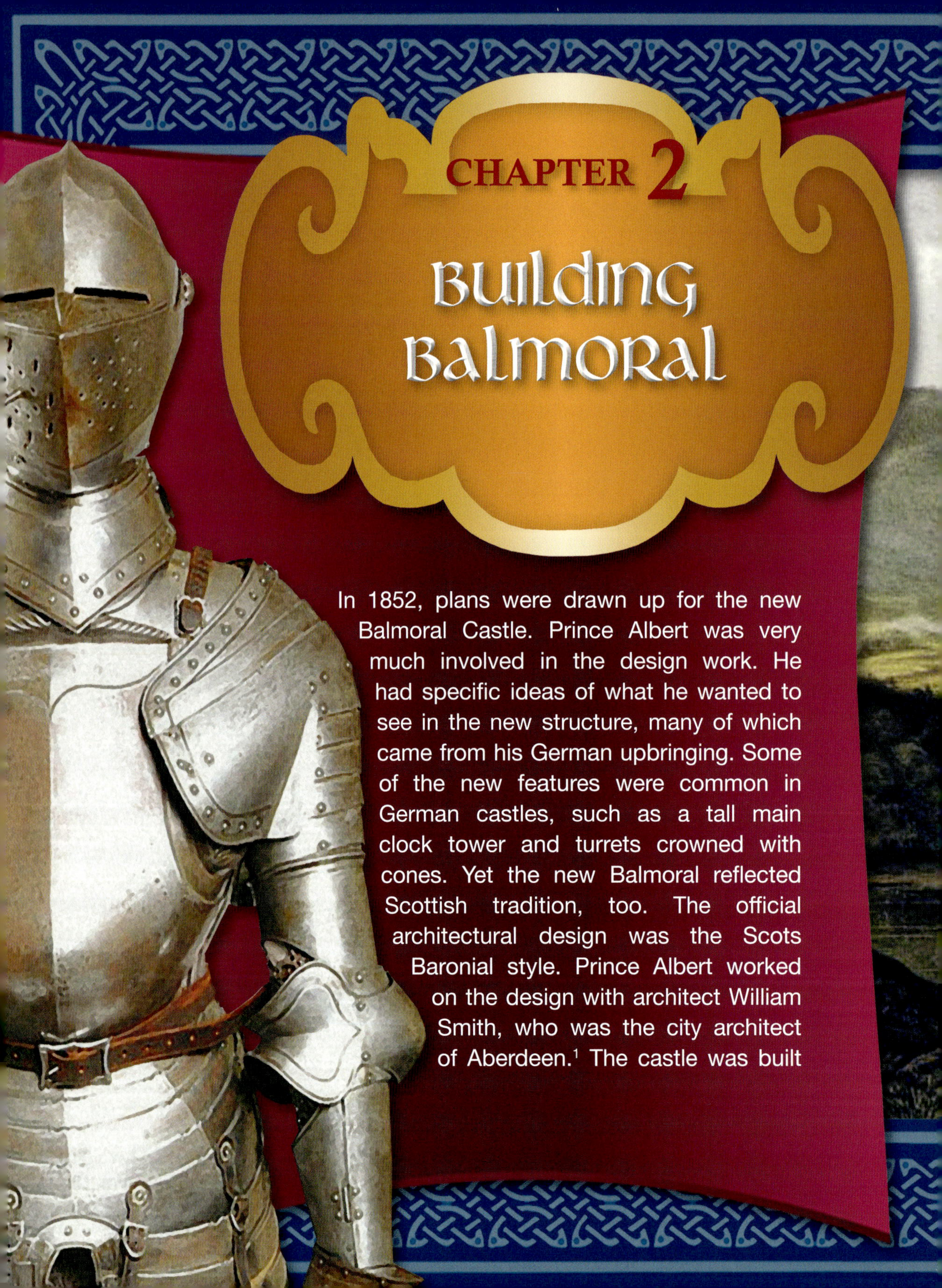

CHAPTER 2

Building Balmoral

In 1852, plans were drawn up for the new Balmoral Castle. Prince Albert was very much involved in the design work. He had specific ideas of what he wanted to see in the new structure, many of which came from his German upbringing. Some of the new features were common in German castles, such as a tall main clock tower and turrets crowned with cones. Yet the new Balmoral reflected Scottish tradition, too. The official architectural design was the Scots Baronial style. Prince Albert worked on the design with architect William Smith, who was the city architect of Aberdeen.[1] The castle was built

The Balmoral Estate was first home to Sir William Drummond in 1390 and also owned by King Robert II (1371–1390).

entirely of silver-gray granite that was quarried from the property's Glen Gelder area.

It was raining on September 28, 1853, when an official ceremony was supposed to take place at Balmoral. At this ceremony, Queen Victoria and the rest of the royal family would start the construction process by laying the castle's cornerstone. Luckily—according to the queen's journal—the rain stopped around 2:00 P.M. and the sky became bright and sunny.

The ceremony went along as planned. Around 3:00 P.M., the royal family emerged from the old castle and made their way to the new castle's construction site. The first stone for the foundation was suspended in the air with heavy ropes. Underneath the stone, a small hole was dug where a time capsule would be placed.

To start the ceremony, Reverend Anderson gave a prayer asking for a blessing on the construction project. Then the queen signed a document that verified the date of the castle's official groundbreaking. The rest of the royal family then signed the document underneath the queen's name. The document was rolled into a tube and, along with some coins from the era, was placed in a glass bottle. A cork was twisted into the bottle's opening to properly seal it, and the architect placed it into the cavity below the stone. After a layer of soil was gently sprinkled on top of the bottle to fill the hole, the stone was lowered into place. The workers adjusted the stone to make sure it was properly leveled, then the queen ceremoniously tapped the stone with a mallet and declared that it was officially in place. Immediately, bagpipe music began to play and the workers cheered.

The rest of the day was spent in celebration, with Highland games on the lawn, toasts to the royal family, and a grand feast and ball for the workers in the evening.[2] Work on the castle would officially begin the following morning, but that night was a time for revelry.

It took three years to complete the new castle. During that time, the royal family still vacationed in Scotland at least once a year, and when they did, they stayed in the old castle. When most of the new castle was complete in 1855, the family moved in. The first time they entered the hall of the new castle, some of the workers gently tossed an old shoe in after

them. This unusual gesture was a Scottish tradition—it was supposed to bring good luck to the royal family and to anyone else who lived in the castle.

The queen wrote in her journal about the first time she saw the new castle. "The house is charming," she said, "the rooms delightful; the furniture, papers, everything perfection."[3] She loved her husband very much and she adored the castle that he designed and had built for their family.

The next fall when the family came up for their annual visit on August 30, the new castle was completed and the old castle had been torn down. A stone from the old castle, which had originally been by the front door, was left in its place as a memorial. It remains on the front lawn of the new Balmoral Castle. Visitors can find it by starting out near the main clock tower and then taking approximately 100 steps toward the middle of the lawn.

The clock tower

The royal family was absolutely delighted with their new home. The exterior was so enchanting that it felt as if they were stepping into a fairy tale. The gardens, woods, and nearby River Dee made the place a charming retreat.

The Queen's Drawing Room, 1857

The interior of Balmoral was just as distinctive. Probably nowhere else in the world was there a castle decorated nearly entirely with tartans, or plaid. If any fabric can define a group of people, tartans can and do when it comes to the Scottish. Because of the strong tie between tartans and Scottish culture, Prince Albert wanted to use this special fabric in as much of the castle's interior design as possible. He chose three main tartans for the home: red Royal Stewart tartan; green Hunting Stewart tartan; and green, blue, and red Stewart Victoria tartan. The first two were used for the carpets throughout the castle and the last was used for the castle's curtains and upholstery. Everywhere a person looked there was tartan, tartan, and more tartan. Even the royal family, when they stayed during vacations, wore tartan of some kind. The workers were also required to wear tartan clothing.[4]

The interior of Balmoral was decorated with antlers and deer heads. One of the main activities at Balmoral was hunting—so it made sense to decorate the castle with a "hunting lodge" theme. Prince Albert insisted on this motif. He wasn't trying to design a palace, but rather a country abode for hunting. For that reason, he made sure there were no expensive oil paintings hanging on the walls and no opulent decorations of any kind. He just wanted Balmoral to be a comfortable country-style Scottish retreat for his family, a place where they could escape the rigors of royal life.[5]

When the Windsor family walks through the front door of Balmoral, they are greeted by stag heads.

HIGHLAND BAGPIPES

The bagpipe is one of the oldest instruments in the world. Its country of origin is unknown. However, the instrument was likely invented by the ancient Egyptians who lived along the Nile River. About 2,000 years ago, it is believed that the Romans brought the instrument into Scotland, and it has been an important part of the culture ever since. The bagpipe was used both as a folk instrument and as a military instrument. There are about 70 different types of bagpipes in the world: Irish, French, Hungarian, Chinese, Turkish, Polish, Spanish, and North African to name a few.

The bagpipe has many parts: the blowpipe, the drone pipes, the bag, and the chanter. To play, the musician fills the bag with air by blowing into the blowpipe. When the drones chime in, the musician knows that the bag is full. Then the player places a little pressure on the bag so that the drones rest on his or her shoulder. When the drones are in place, the musician blows into the blowpipe again to tap the chanter. The chanter is a long pipe that has small holes cut into it. It looks like a recorder or flutaphone. Finger placement on the chanter determines which musical notes are played. While the bagpiper is playing a tune on the chanter, he or she is constantly blowing air into the blowpipe to fill the bag. Playing the bagpipe is both difficult, but fun. It takes a lot of practice to play it well.

Musicians who learn how to play the bagpipe often join bagpipe bands. These bands consist of several bagpipers and drummers. They play in parades, competitions, and special cultural celebrations.

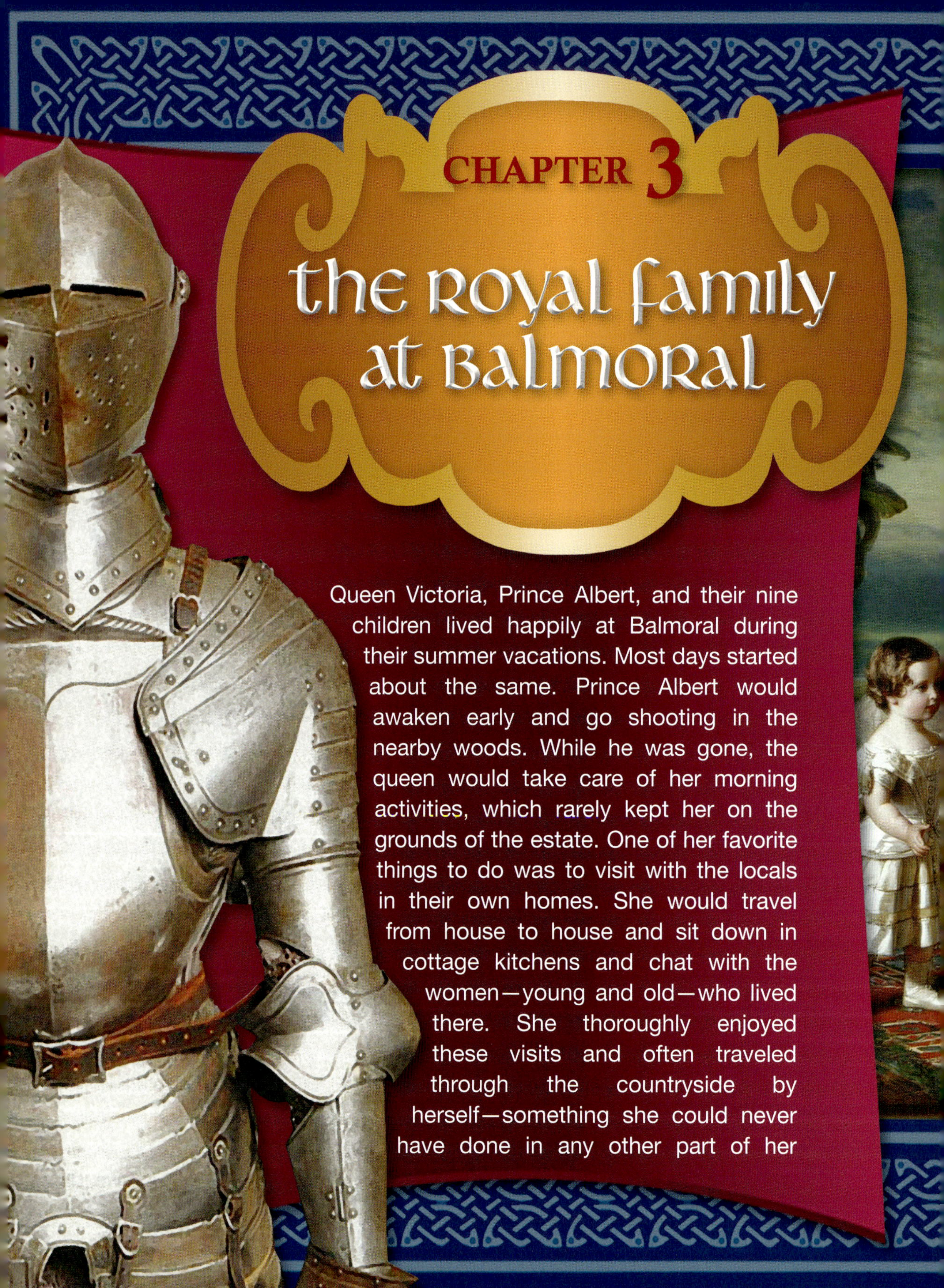

CHAPTER 3

The Royal Family at Balmoral

Queen Victoria, Prince Albert, and their nine children lived happily at Balmoral during their summer vacations. Most days started about the same. Prince Albert would awaken early and go shooting in the nearby woods. While he was gone, the queen would take care of her morning activities, which rarely kept her on the grounds of the estate. One of her favorite things to do was to visit with the locals in their own homes. She would travel from house to house and sit down in cottage kitchens and chat with the women—young and old—who lived there. She thoroughly enjoyed these visits and often traveled through the countryside by herself—something she could never have done in any other part of her

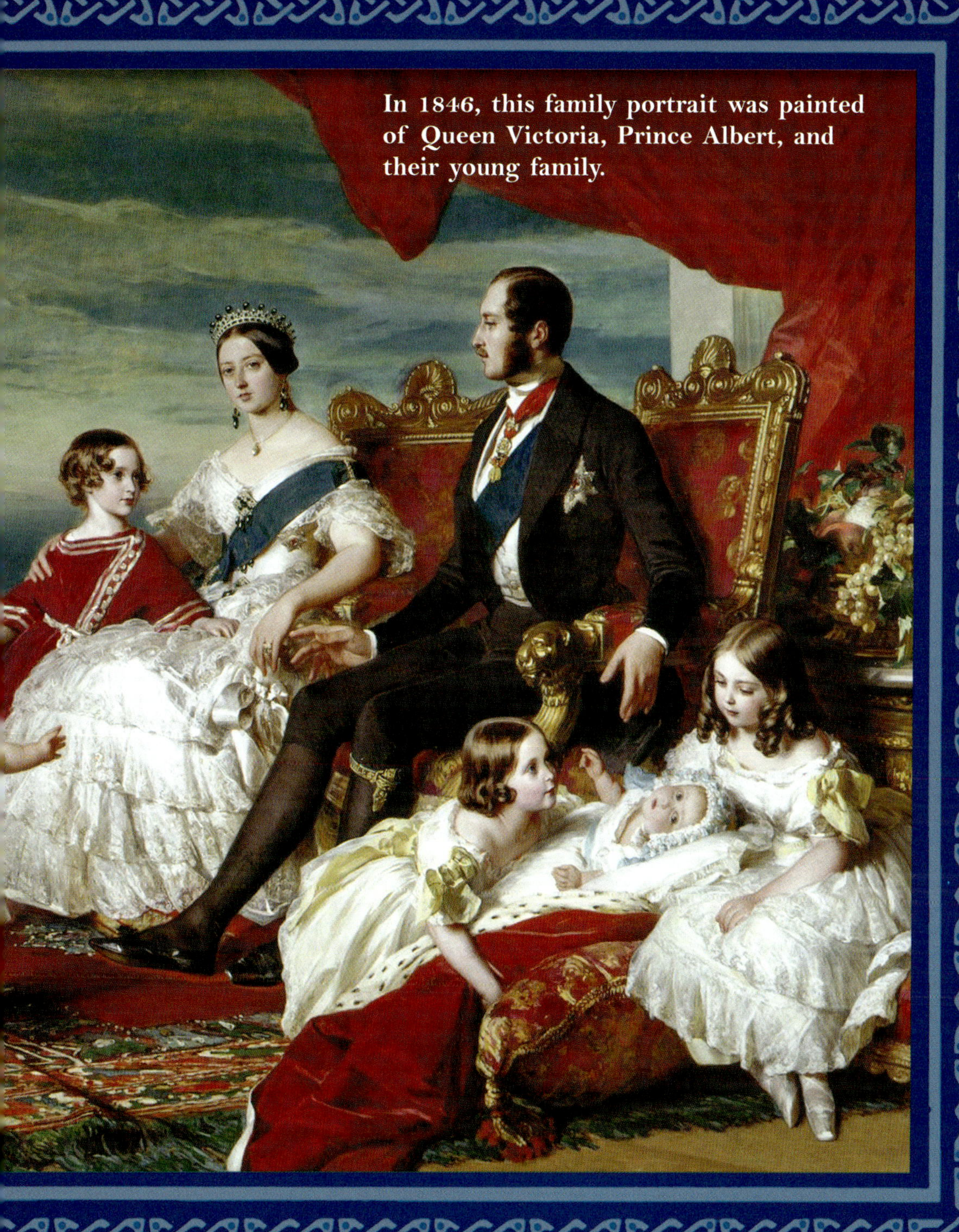
In 1846, this family portrait was painted of Queen Victoria, Prince Albert, and their young family.

Queen Victoria in 1860

kingdom. Around noon, both the prince and the queen would return to Balmoral. Sometimes they would eat in the castle with their children. Other times they'd take their lunch on the road and have a picnic. They'd spread out a tartan blanket over the pink heather and eat while looking out over the beautiful countryside. In the afternoons, the royal couple would go hiking or driving together. The evenings were generally spent at the castle. Sometimes the family would have private dance lessons where they would learn the traditional Scottish reels from Highland dancing masters.[1] Other times, they'd play billiards and chess and other games.

The children had their own activities. They often started their day by eating a big bowl of porridge, followed by oatcakes. Then they had daily lessons with their tutors. They studied sketching, painting, photography, and gardening. Soldiers drilled the boys to improve their physical abilities and strength. Later in the day, the children were allowed to go out and play with the local children who lived nearby.[2] This was also something that would rarely, if ever, have happened anywhere else in the kingdom. Balmoral was indeed a special place where the royal family could be free to associate with the average everyday person and feel like they were almost one of them.

Prince Albert

In 1861, tragedy struck the royal family. Prince Albert became seriously ill and there was nothing the doctors could do to save his life. As he lay dying in his bed at Windsor Castle, Queen Victoria read to him from one of Sir Walter Scott's novels, *Peveril of the Peak.*[3] Scott's descriptions of the couple's beloved Scottish landscape were the last words Prince Albert ever heard. He passed away at age 42 on December 14, 1861.

Albert's death was devastating to Queen Victoria; she adored him and never really moved on. For the next 40 years of her life, she wore black mourning clothes. She wanted to show the world that she still grieved the loss of her dear husband—and became known as the Widow of Windsor.

Queen Victoria's personal servant, John Brown, became a close friend of hers. They are captured together in this image from 1868.

Every year, just as she had done with Albert, Victoria continued to spend time at Balmoral. She actually spent more and more time in Scotland, most likely because of the good memories she had there. Albert had designed and built the castle. The couple had loved the Scottish countryside. When she went there, she could remember the good times. Since Victoria was spending less time in London, her ministers had to travel the many-day's journey to Balmoral in order for her to take care of government matters. Not all of the ministers loved Balmoral or the Scottish Highlands as much as she did; it was not always a pleasant experience for them to travel there.

When Queen Victoria passed away in 1901, the crown—and along with it, Balmoral Castle—went to her eldest son, Edward VII. Even though King Edward VII had spent his childhood and adult years going to Balmoral with his parents, his siblings, and his own children, he really didn't care for it as much as his parents did. Edward VII was more of an urbanite—he loved everything about the big city: the parties, the social functions, the arts and culture. Edward wasn't fond of hunting or fishing or any other similar outdoor activities—so Balmoral Castle was really not that interesting to him. During his nine-year reign, Edward VII stayed in London as much as possible and avoided Balmoral.

The next several generations of British monarchs all had differing feelings about Balmoral. Some loved it just as much as Victoria and Albert had, and some cared just as little as Edward VII.

Edward's son, King George V, agreed with his grandparents' philosophy. He thought Balmoral was one of the most delightful places on Earth. He adored hunting and fishing and everything else that Balmoral had to offer. He loved the Highland culture, the bagpipes, and the food of Scotland. George V reigned for 26 years. When he passed away, his eldest son, David, inherited the throne as King Edward VIII.

There must certainly be something in the name of Edward, because King Edward VIII didn't like Balmoral any more than his grandfather, King Edward VII. Edward VIII belonged to a socialite crowd. These friends preferred going to fancy parties in ornate palaces; they didn't have any interest in visiting a tartan-filled hunting lodge. Edward VIII felt exactly the same way as his

King Edward and Wallis Simpson, 1936

friends. At one of the only functions hosted at Balmoral, one of King Edward's friends remarked that the "awful tartan" adornments just had to go!

Less than a year into his reign, Edward VIII decided he had had enough of being king. He wanted to marry someone of whom the family did not approve, so he was forced to abdicate, or give up, the crown. The crown went to his brother, Albert George, who was from that point on known as King George VI.

King George VI and his wife, Elizabeth—who in most recent times was known as the Queen Mum, or Queen Mother—adored Balmoral. They often brought their children there for the same holiday retreats that Victoria and Albert had taken their children. King George had also gone on these retreats with his own family when his father, George V, was king. Elizabeth, the couple's oldest daughter, spent many happy years there with her family when she was a child. Eventually, she would be crowned Queen Elizabeth II—the same Queen Elizabeth who was the reigning monarch of Great Britain well into the twenty-first century.

King George and Elizabeth the Queen Mother

Elizabeth II was the first queen to inherit the throne since Victoria. And just like her great-great-grandmother, Elizabeth loved everything about

Phillip proposed to Elizabeth at Balmoral. The castle still remains a special spot for them and their family.

Balmoral. From the time she was a small child, Elizabeth adored the times that her family spent at their castle in the Scottish Highlands. She loved the picnics on the tartan blankets, the pony rides through the heather, and the visits with the locals who lived near the castle. Elizabeth's adoration of Balmoral made it the perfect place for Prince Phillip to propose marriage to her in 1946.[4] More than sixty years later, Elizabeth and Phillip were still bringing their family to Balmoral to carry on the traditions that the monarchy had started so many years before. Their children, Charles (Prince of Wales), Anne (Princess Royal), Andrew (Duke of York), and Edward (Earl of Wessex), all share the same love for Balmoral as their parents. They often vacation in Balmoral with their children and grandchildren.

HIGHLAND PONIES

Highland pony

Highland ponies are native to Scotland. These compact horses come in many different colors: some are gray-brown, some are pure white (which is also considered gray), some are black, some are yellowish tan, some are chestnut. Some even have zebra-like stripes on their legs—but any white marking other than a star on the forehead disqualifies an animal from the breed. These ponies have a coarse and dense winter coat to keep them warm in the windy, cold Highland weather. In the spring, they shed their winter coats and bear a smooth, shiny coat through the warmer summer months.

Originally, Highland ponies were workhorses. They helped plow the fields, haul timber, and pull wagons. These animals are still used as workhorses, but they are also used for pleasure riding and especially jumping. When the royal family visits Balmoral, they ride their Highland ponies into the forests, moors, and heather-clad foothills. They also ride them on hunting expeditions.

Queen Elizabeth II received her first Highland pony when she was four years old. It was a gift from her grandfather, King George V. She became an instant fan of horseback riding, and eventually became quite good at it. In the 1940s, she won a competition at the Royal Windsor Show with one of her Highland ponies named Windsor Gypsy. The descendants of Windsor Gypsy are still riding, playing, and working at Balmoral Castle.[5]

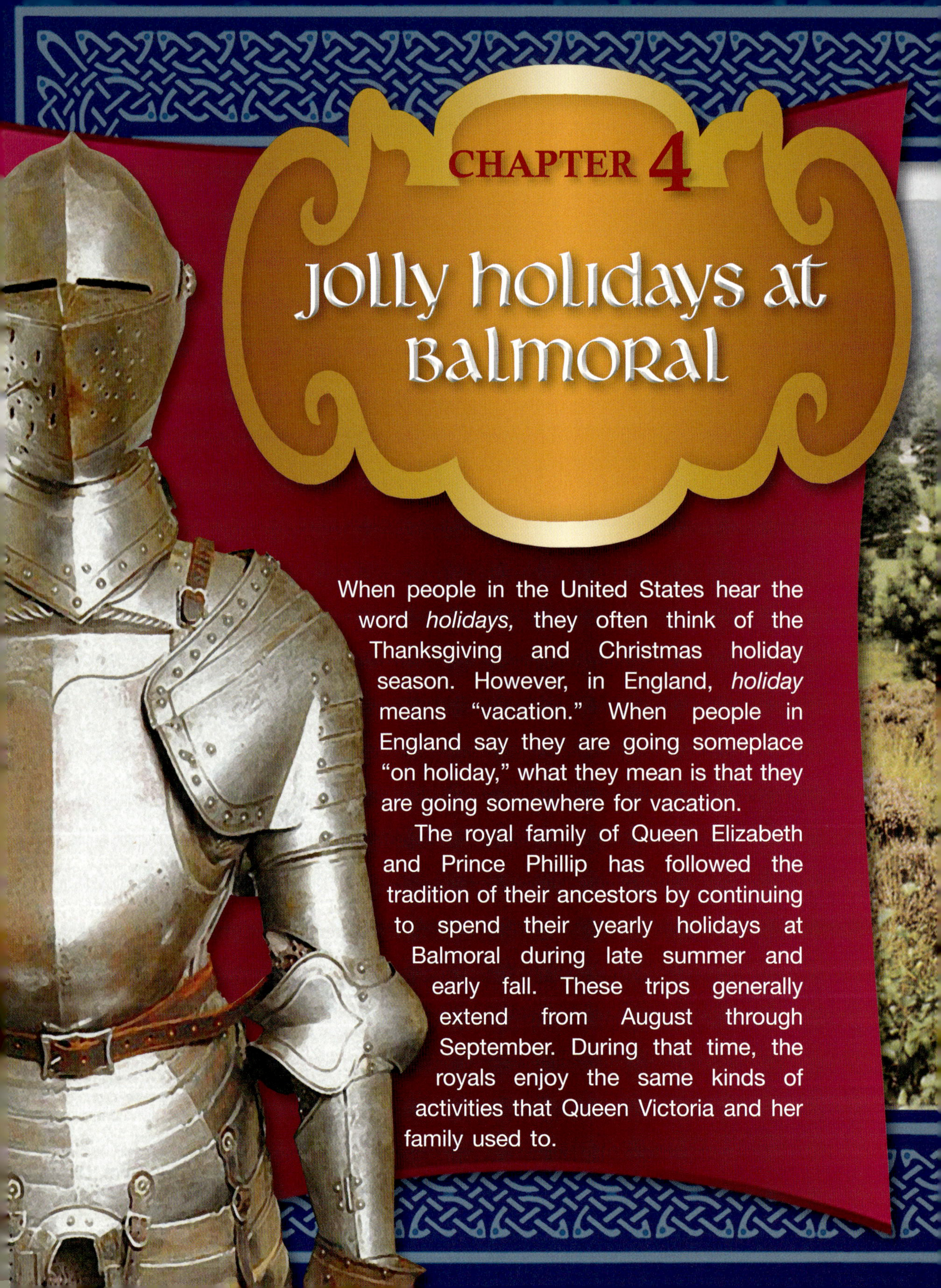

CHAPTER 4

Jolly Holidays at Balmoral

When people in the United States hear the word *holidays,* they often think of the Thanksgiving and Christmas holiday season. However, in England, *holiday* means "vacation." When people in England say they are going someplace "on holiday," what they mean is that they are going somewhere for vacation.

The royal family of Queen Elizabeth and Prince Phillip has followed the tradition of their ancestors by continuing to spend their yearly holidays at Balmoral during late summer and early fall. These trips generally extend from August through September. During that time, the royals enjoy the same kinds of activities that Queen Victoria and her family used to.

Queen Elizabeth II loves riding horses through the Highlands at Balmoral.

Preparing a ride at Balmoral

The schedule at Balmoral is not as rigid as it is in the queen's other residences, but it still has some order to it. First of all, the queen is awakened every morning, not by the sound of an alarm clock, but by the sound of a bagpiper playing outside her window at 9:00 A.M. She lounges with breakfast in bed, then she gets ready for the day.[1]

The royal family enjoys many different types of daytime activities. They stroll the grounds of the castle and admire the gardens and green spaces. They ride horseback through the heather. They hunt in the forests. They fish in the River Dee. They ride into the surrounding villages and shop at the marketplaces. The queen is even known to drive herself around the grounds in an SUV with her beloved corgis by her side. The family also enjoys picnics. On these particular outings, Queen Elizabeth usually tosses together a salad while Prince Phillip cooks on a small portable grill. Generally, he grills venison from a family hunting trip, beef or sausage from the cattle raised at Balmoral, or salmon from a family fishing adventure. Once the food is prepared, they all sit on large tartan blankets and enjoy their meal together. These types of outings would not be possible in other parts of the kingdom. In Balmoral, the royals are able to get away from it all and enjoy life without the nuisance of paparazzi or other people to bother them.

In the evenings, the family enjoys quiet time in the warmth of the castle, usually in front of the flickering flames of the fireplace. Though it's late summer, the weather can be very chilly in the Highlands. The family often plays cards, bridge, or charades. Sometimes they'll put together a jigsaw puzzle or play a game of chess. Other times, they'll listen to one of the family members play the piano. This is the family's time just to spend together and talk. The royal family is so busy—each member of the family has responsibilities that fill most of their time throughout the rest of the year—that these few months at Balmoral are priceless. They give the family some time to get reacquainted and catch up on all the family news.

Daytime dress at Balmoral is always casual—and some kind of tartan is usually worn. The queen generally wears a dress or skirt made out of tartan material. Prince Phillip often wears a kilt. Their children do likewise. Now that their grandchildren are older, though, it seems that fewer of the younger generation are wearing the traditional Scottish attire. During the evening, the clothing is generally more formal, especially when the family has invited guests to the castle for dinner.

One of the family's favorite things to do while at Balmoral is to attend the Braemar Highland Games, which are held the first Saturday in September. These games have been a tradition in this part of Scotland for more than 900

The caber toss is one of the oldest competitions in Scotland. It is still played at the Highland Games.

Many different bagpipe bands from all over Scotland come together to perform at the Highland Games.

years, and they were particularly popular with Victoria and Albert. At this event, athletes and musicians come together to celebrate Highland culture. The athletes compete in various games such as the caber toss, stone put, and hammer throw. Bagpipe bands compete in several events, including solo piping, drumming competitions, and small ensembles. All of the bands that come to the event generally perform together for the opening and closing grand parades. Every year, the queen officially presides as the chieftain of the games.[2]

HIGHLAND CATTLE

Just like Texas has a special kind of cattle—the Texas Longhorn—so does Scotland's Highlands. These cows, called Highland cattle, have been raised in the Highlands since the 1700s. They have long brownish red hair that grows in two separate layers. This keeps them warm in the cold, windy, Highland climate. Their short, pointy horns are about 8 inches long.

Highland cattle are known to be friendly. They are also curious about the things and people around them, acting a lot like friendly dogs. They will eat a wide variety of vegetation, which is helpful when searching for food in the varied landscapes of the Highlands.[3]

In 1954, Queen Elizabeth II announced that she was going to raise her own Highland cattle at Balmoral. Of course, she didn't personally raise them: she had expert cattle ranchers to do the job. Yet, when she came on her annual visits, she definitely spent time meeting with her ranchers and inspecting the herds. She still does today.

In 2013, one of the queen's Highland bulls, Ruaridh, won a competition. This four-year-old bull came in top of its class at the City of Glasgow International Highland Cattle Show in Scotland.[4]

Highland cattle

CHAPTER 5

Balmoral today

When Prince Albert purchased Balmoral in the 1840s, the estate covered only about 11,000 acres. Over the years, successive monarchs purchased additional land, bringing the land area to approximately 50,000 acres. That's almost five times the size of the original property.

On the estate, there are 2,500 acres of pine woodlands in the Ballochbuie Forest. It is the largest area of Caledonian forest left in all of Great Britain. A very old forest, it is home to red deer, black and red grouse, red squirrels, and birds of prey. In 1878, a logging company wanted to come into the forest and cut down all the trees for timber. Queen Victoria wanted to protect the forest. She bought the property and added it to the estate.[1]

Balmoral is just as beautiful today as it was when Queen Victoria and Prince Albert first constructed it.

About 250 acres of the land at Balmoral is farmed by the castle staff, and about 185 acres is leased to neighboring farmers. Most of the rest of the land cannot be used for farming or gardening because it is either too mountainous, covered in dense forests, or is in swampy areas called moors. There are seven small mountains, called munros; they are between 1,000 and 3,000 feet high.

Balmoral is a working estate. Even though the royal family only goes there for two months of the year, people still need to stay at the castle and take care of it when the royal family isn't there. These employees care for the castle, the grounds, the farmland, and the animals on the estate. They also help people who visit the castle during the tourist season. About 50

Horses roam the property at Balmoral and are a favorite mode of transportation for the queen when she visits.

The Balmoral vegetable garden supplies the royal family with fresh produce during the summer holiday season.

people work at Balmoral full-time. Another 50 to 100 workers come to the castle when the royal family is in residence.

Balmoral is the royal family's private home. Because of that, the castle and grounds are open to tourists only at certain times of the year: from April 1 until July 31. About 85,000 people visit the castle during that four-month period, which is an average of 5,300 per week. During that time, the entire house isn't open for tours. Visitors are only allowed to enter the castle's grand ballroom, which is the largest room in the castle and the same hall where the annual Ghillies Ball is held. The rest of the castle, since it includes the private belongings of the queen and her family, is off-limits to the general public.

The ballroom has been turned into a sort of museum, showcasing some of the royal family's memorabilia. There are silver statues by Sir Joseph

Prince Albert statue

Edgar Boehm, who was a royal sculptor for the monarchy during Queen Victoria's reign. There are also paintings by artists Sir Edwin Henry Landseer and Carl Haag. Landseer is best known for his horse, dog, and stag paintings—these types of paintings have been a favorite type of artwork to be displayed at Balmoral since Victorian times. Haag is best known for his landscapes and portraitures. His painting titled *Evening in Balmoral* shows Queen Victoria and one of her children looking at a stag that Prince Albert had just brought back from the hunt. In addition to the paintings and sculptures, the ballroom has on display the royal family's Minton china, a collection of Victoria's royal dresses, and random furniture pieces and artifacts used at Balmoral.

There may be only one room to view in the castle, but that doesn't mean a visit to Balmoral will be short. On the contrary, a person could spend an entire day there and still not be able to see everything that the estate has to offer. One popular activity at Balmoral is going on a safari tour. On these tours, visitors ride in an SUV through

The Caledonian pine forest

various places on the estate, including the Caledonian pine forest, the heather-covered hillsides, and the castle's parklands and gardens. This tour is so popular that visitors have to book reservations for it well in advance.

Other visitors take walking tours with a park ranger as their guide. The park rangers are very knowledgeable about the area, so the tour includes interesting stories and facts about the castle and the grounds. They often take people up to the cairns. These are traditional Scottish monuments that are made by piling stones into a pyramid. A large cairn was built by the royal family when Balmoral was first purchased. Smaller cairns were built for each of the royal children. When Prince Albert died, Queen Victoria had a very large cairn built in his memory. It's a bit of a hike up to the cairns, but well worth the journey.

If walking is too slow for you, then how about a good run through Balmoral? Every April, there are two full days of racing through the roads and trails of the castle's estate. Some races meander through the forests and foothills. Some are just for grownups. Some are just for kids. Some are for tweens and teens. Others include both runners and athletes in wheelchairs. Runners can also come to Balmoral at other times of the year for a Running the Highlands weekend, where they run with personal trainers and listen to special presentations by expert runners.

Other activities to be enjoyed at Balmoral include fishing and golfing. When Prince Charles stays at Balmoral, he fishes in the River Dee. Visitors can fish on the river, too. Fly-fishing is the norm there—but all fishing is catch-and-release. The fish have to be returned to the river to help conserve the region's natural resources.

When the queen comes on her annual holiday, she spends part of her time on her personal golf course. During the tourist season, visitors can golf there too. They have to make reservations in advance, though, since many people want to golf on the royal course.

Visitors can also stay overnight at Balmoral—not inside the castle itself, but in the cottages on the property. These cottages are open even when the royal family is on their annual holiday. Some cottage guests have reported that they've been out enjoying the gardens and lawns at Balmoral when they actually ran into the queen while she was taking her corgis for a walk. Some cottages are very close to the castle, while others are farther away. Some cottages can fit up to 13 people while others can fit only six or seven. Staying at Balmoral is a once-in-a-lifetime experience. When else could you say that you stayed on the same estate as the royal family?

For those who don't have the opportunity to visit Balmoral right now, there are plenty of other ways to learn about the castle. People can learn about it by reading books (like this one), by looking up the official website on the Internet, and by watching documentaries online or on television. There are also guided virtual tour apps available online that will let you stroll through the grounds via your smart phone, tablet, or other handheld device.

Balmoral is an enchanting place that is rich with history. It is just as beautiful now as it was in Queen Victoria's and Prince Albert's time. Take the time to visit, either in person or through books or media. You'll be glad you did.

ROYAL PETS

Queen and Corgi

Since the seventeenth century, dogs have been the favorite pets of the royal family. They have been featured in many of the family's formal portraits since that time period. Some of the pets have been considered part of the family.

King Edward VI had a terrier named Caesar. He was greatly loved by the king and even followed the king's funeral procession when the king died.

Queen Elizabeth loves corgis. When she was a young girl, her father—King George VI—bought a corgi named Dookie. This dog proved to be a favorite companion of Elizabeth and her sister, Princess Margaret. From that point on, Queen Elizabeth has always had at least one pet corgi. She often takes her animals with her to Balmoral and cares for them herself as often as she is able. They fly on the plane together to get to Balmoral and then they go on hikes, walks, and outings in the beautiful Highland countryside.

Queen Victoria's favorite dog was Noble, who was a collie. When he died at Balmoral Castle in 1887, the queen established a pet cemetery on the castle grounds.[2] They buried Noble there and gave him a special monument. On top of the monument is a bronze statue of the dog. On the bottom of the monument are the words:

> Noble by name by nature noble too
> Faithful companion sympathetic true
> His remains are interred here[3]

It is estimated that around 100 royal pets have been buried at Balmoral since Queen Victoria established this special pet cemetery.[4] The royal pets—including one of Queen Elizabeth's corgi Monty, who died just after the London Summer Olympics in 2012—all get their own special monument or headstone in the cemetery.

Introduction

1. "Then Queen confides some 'trade secrets.'"

   https://www.youtube.com/watch?v=4wknuHbv6J4

Chapter 1

1. Victoria, Queen of Great Britain, *Leaves from the Journal of Our Life in the Highlands: From 1848–1861.* (London: Smith, Elder and Co., 1877), p. 3.
2. Victoria, p.16.

Chapter 2

1. Balmoral: Scottish home to the Royal Family.

   http://www.balmoralcastle.com/about.htm
2. Victoria, Queen of Great Britain, *Leaves from the Journal of Our Life in the Highlands: From 1848–1861.* (London: Smith, Elder and Co., 1877), pp. 106–107.
3. Victoria, p. 109.
4. "Balmoral Castle" Documentary 2 of 4, https://www.youtube.com/watch?v=ogqI5Ok2sxo
5. Patricia Robertson Lindsay, *Recollections of a Royal Parish.* (London: John Murray, 1902), p. 39.

Chapter 3

1. Millicent Garrett Fawcett, *Life of Her Majesty Queen Victoria,* (Boston: LIttle, Brown, and Company, 1907), pp.137–139.
2. Mrs. Frank Pope Humphrey, *The Queen at Balmoral,* (London: T. Fischer Unwin, 1893), p. 165.
3. "Balmoral Castle" Documentary 2 of 4, https://www.youtube.com/watch?v=ogqI5Ok2sxo
4. Sally Bedell Smith, "Love and Majesty," *Vanity Fair,* http://www.vanityfair.com/society/2012/01/queen-elizabeth-201201

5. Steve White, "Queen Bans Balmoral visitors from trekking on her ponies—because riders are too fat," *Mirror,* February 24, 2012, http://www.mirror.co.uk/news/uk-news/queen-bans-balmoral-visitors-trekking-741660. Accessed August 16, 2014.

Chapter 4

1. Michelle Green and Elizabeth Terry, "Highland Fling," *People,* September 19, 1994, p. 214.
2. "The Scottish Summer Respite," *British Heritage,* January 2013, pp.16–17.
3. "Highland Cattle," Roaming Farm LLC website.
4. Kelby McNally, "The Queen's Highland bull wins competition and creates YouTube hit," October 2, 2013, http://www.express.co.uk/news/royal/433884/The-Queen-s-Highland-bull-wins-competition-and-creates-youtube-hit.

Chapter 5

1. "Queen Victoria's Homes." PBS website.

   http://www.pbs.org/empires/victoria/majesty/home.html
2. Petter Larsson, "Queen's 13-year-old corgi Monty who appeared in Olympics Opening Ceremony dies," September 11, 2012, http://www.tntmagazine.com/news/london/queens-13-year-old-corgi-monty-who-appeared-in-olympics-opening-ceremony-dies.
3. "Family Pets," *The Official website of the British Monarchy,*

   http://www.royal.gov.uk/TheRoyalHousehold/RoyalAnimals/Familypets.aspx
4. Green, p. 214.

Books

Boyer, Crispin. *National Geographic Kids Everything Castles: Capture These Facts, Photos, and Fun to Be King of the Castle!* Washington, DC: National Geographic Children's Books, 2011.

Gigliotti, Jim. *Who Was Queen Victoria?* New York: Grosset & Dunlap, 2014.

Gravett, Christopher. *Castle.* New York: DK Eyewitness Books, 2008.

Kiehm, Eve Begley. *B is for Bagpipes.* Ann Arbor, MI: Sleeping Bear Press, 2010.

Marshall, H. E. *Our Island Story: A History of Britain for Boys and Girls, from the Romans to Queen Victoria.* CreateSpace Independent Publishing Platform, 2014.

Waldron, Melanie. Scotland (Countries Around the World). Mankato, MN: Heinemann-Raintree, 2011.

Works Consulted

"Balmoral Castle." Documentary 2 of 4. https://www.youtube.com/watch?v=ogqI5Ok2sxo. Accessed August 16, 2014.

Balmoral: Scottish home to the Royal Family. http://www.balmoralcastle.com/about.htm. Accessed August 16, 2014.

"Family Pet. *The Official website of the British Monarchy.* http://www.royal.gov.uk/TheRoyalHousehold/RoyalAnimals/Familypets.aspx.

Fawcett, Millicent Garrett. *Life of Her Majesty Queen Victoria.* Boston: Little, Brown, and Company, 1907.

Green, Michelle, and Elizabeth Terry. "Highland Fling." *People.* September 19, 1994.

"Highland Cattle." Roaming Farm LLC website. Accessed August 16, 2014.

Humphrey, Mrs. Frank Pope. *The Queen at Balmoral.* London: T. Fischer Unwin, 1893.

Larsson, Petter. "Queen's 13-year-old corgi Monty who appeared in Olympics Opening Ceremony dies." September 11, 2012. http://www.tntmagazine.com/news/london/queens-13-year-old-corgi-monty-who-appeared-in-olympics-opening-ceremony dies. Accessed August 16, 2014.

Lindsay, Patricia Robertson. *Recollections of a Royal Parish.* London: John Murray, 1902.

McNally, Kelby. "The Queen's Highland bull wins competition and creates YouTube hit." October 2, 2013. http://www.express.co.uk/news/royal/433884/The-Queen-s-Highland-bull-wins-competition-and-creates-youtube-hit. Accessed August 16, 2014.

"Queen Victoria's Homes." PBS website.

http://www.pbs.org/empires/victoria/majesty/home.html. Accessed August 16, 2014.

"The Scottish Summer Respite." *British Heritage.* January 2013.

Smith, Sally Bedell. "Love and Majesty." *Vanity Fair.* January 2012. http://www.vanityfair.com/society/2012/01/queen-elizabeth-201201. Accessed August 16, 2014.

"Then Queen confides some 'trade secrets.'" https://www.youtube.com/watch?v=4wknuHbv6J4. Accessed August 16, 2014.

Victoria, Queen of Great Britain. *Leaves from the Journal of Our Life in the Highlands: From 1848–1861.* London: Smith, Elder and Co., 1877.

White, Steve. "Queen Bans Balmoral visitors from trekking on her ponies—because riders are too fat." *Mirror.* February 24, 2012. http://www.mirror.co.uk/news/uk-news/queen-bans-balmoral-visitors-trekking-741660. Accessed August 16, 2014.

On the Internet

Balmoral Castle
http://www.balmoralcastle.com/about.htm

Balmoral Castle, Scotland
http://www.visitscotland.com/en-us/info/see-do/balmoral-castle-p245771

BBC: History for Kids
http://www.bbc.co.uk/history/forkids/

The Official Website of the British Monarchy
http://www.royal.gov.uk/

Time for Kids: England Timeline
http://www.timeforkids.com/destination/england/history-timeline

PHOTO CREDITS: Pp. 8-9–Alden Chadwick. Cover and all other photos—cc-by-sa-2.0. Every measure has been taken to find all copyright holders of material used in this book. In the event any mistakes or omissions have happened within, attempts to correct them will be made in future editions of the book.

Glossary

accordion (uh-KOR-dee-uhn)—A box-shaped musical instrument that is held in the arms and played by squeezing the box in and out while pressing the buttons or keys on the piano-like keyboard.

bagpipe (BAG-pipe)—A musical instrument held in the arms that involves filling a bag with air and squeezing the bag slightly to make a sound come out of three pipes. Music is played on a chanter similar to a recorder or flutaphone.

candelabra (KAN-duhl-AHH-bruh)—A fancy candlestick holder that holds more than one candle at a time.

carriage (KAIR-ihj)—A vehicle that is usually pulled by animals like horses.

corner stone (KOR-ner STONE)—The stone that is placed at the corner of a newly-constructed building.

feather bonnets (FEH-ther BAH-nets)—Tall hats covered in black feathers that are often worn by bagpipers.

groundbreaking (GROUND BRAYK-ing)—A special ceremony held to begin the construction of an important building.

mallet (MAHL-uht)—A tool that is similar to a hammer but has a head that is usually made out of rubber or wood.

paparazzi (PAH-pur-AHZEE)—Photographers that are known to follow around famous people trying to catch candid (unposed) photos.

porridge (PORE-ihj)—A cereal popular in Scotland that is made out of oats.

reel (REEL)—A special kind of organized dance routine that often includes many couples.

tartan (TAR-tuhn)—A special kind of fabric that comes in different colors and plaids.

time capsule (TIME KAP-suhl)—A special container of objects that shows what is important at the time a building is constructed.

upholstery (uh-POLE-stree)—Fabric that is used to cover sofas and chairs.

waltz (WAHLTZ)—A special kind of dance that involves certain steps and is completed in couples.

index